D0482136

Dear Parents and Educators,

Welcome to Penguin Young Readers! As parents and educators, you know that each child develops at his or her own pace—in terms of speech, critical thinking, and, of course, reading. Penguin Young Readers recognizes this fact. As a result, each Penguin Young Readers book is assigned a traditional easy-to-read level (1–4) as well as a Guided Reading Level (A–P). Both of these systems will help you choose the right book for your child. Please refer to the back of each book for specific leveling information. Penguin Young Readers features esteemed authors and illustrators, stories about favorite characters, fascinating nonfiction, and more!

Young Cam Jansen and the Speedy Car Mystery

LEVEL **3**

GUIDED READING LEVEL **J**

This book is perfect for a **Transitional Reader** who:
- can read multisyllable and compound words;
- can read words with prefixes and suffixes;
- is able to identify story elements (beginning, middle, end, plot, setting, characters, problem, solution); and
- can understand different points of view.

Here are some **activities** you can do during and after reading this book:
- Picture Clues: Sometimes, pictures can tell you something about the story that is not told in words. After reading the story, look at the pictures on pages 14 and 15 when Ben first notices that Speedy is missing. How can these pictures help you solve the mystery?
- Characters' Feelings: In this story, Danny tells three jokes. Each time he tries to tell a joke, other characters ignore him. Discuss how this might make Danny feel. However, one of Danny's jokes ends up helping Cam solve the mystery of the missing car. Discuss how that might make him feel.

Remember, sharing the love of reading with a child is the best gift you can give!

—Bonnie Bader, EdM
  Penguin Young Readers program

*Penguin Young Readers are leveled by independent reviewers applying the standards developed by Irene Fountas and Gay Su Pinnell in *Matching Books to Readers: Using Leveled Books in Guided Reading*, Heinemann, 1999.

With love to my aunt Edith and
to her children, grandchildren,
and great-grandchildren—DA

To Kathleen Kolb—SN

Penguin Young Readers
Published by the Penguin Group
Penguin Group (USA) Inc., 375 Hudson Street, New York, New York 10014, USA
Penguin Group (Canada), 90 Eglinton Avenue East, Suite 700, Toronto, Ontario M4P 2Y3, Canada
(a division of Pearson Penguin Canada Inc.)
Penguin Books Ltd, 80 Strand, London WC2R 0RL, England
Penguin Ireland, 25 St Stephen's Green, Dublin 2, Ireland (a division of Penguin Books Ltd)
Penguin Group (Australia), 707 Collins Street, Melbourne, Victoria 3008, Australia
(a division of Pearson Australia Group Pty Ltd)
Penguin Books India Pvt Ltd, 11 Community Centre, Panchsheel Park, New Delhi—110 017, India
Penguin Group (NZ), 67 Apollo Drive, Rosedale, Auckland 0632, New Zealand
(a division of Pearson New Zealand Ltd)
Penguin Books, Rosebank Office Park, 181 Jan Smuts Avenue, Parktown North 2193, South Africa
Penguin China, B7 Jaiming Center, 27 East Third Ring Road North,
Chaoyang District, Beijing 100020, China

Penguin Books Ltd, Registered Offices: 80 Strand, London WC2R 0RL, England

Text copyright © 2010 by David A. Adler. Illustrations copyright © 2010 by Susanna Natti. All rights reserved. First published in 2010 by Viking and in 2011 by Puffin Books, imprints of Penguin Group (USA) Inc. Published in 2012 by Penguin Young Readers, an imprint of Penguin Group (USA) Inc., 345 Hudson Street, New York, New York 10014. Manufactured in China.

The Library of Congress has cataloged the Viking edition under the following Control Number:
2009024902

ISBN 978-0-14-241868-0   10 9 8 7 6 5 4

Young Cam Jansen
and the Speedy Car Mystery

by David A. Adler
illustrated by Susanna Natti

Penguin Young Readers
An Imprint of Penguin Group (USA) Inc.

Contents

Chapter 1
What's Green and Jumpy?

"This is Mrs. Kane," Ms. Dee told her class.

"She was my sixth-grade science teacher many years ago."

Mrs. Kane was sitting by the doors to the gym.

"Welcome to the Green Fair," Ms. Dee said.

"My sixth graders will show you what we can all do to keep our earth green."

"Hello, Mrs. Kane," the children said.

"This is Cam Jansen," Ms. Dee said. "She's the girl with the amazing memory."

Eric said, "Cam has pictures in her head of everything she's seen."

Danny said, "And I'm the boy with the jokes in my head. 'What's green and jumpy?'"

"I know all about you," Mrs. Kane told Cam.

"Your real name is Jennifer, but because of those pictures in your head, people called you 'the Camera.' Then 'the Camera' became 'Cam.'"

"What about my joke?" Danny asked.

"Look at me," Mrs. Kane said to Cam.

Cam looked at Mrs. Kane.

Cam blinked her eyes and said, "Click!"

Cam always says, "Click!" when she wants to remember something.

She says it's the sound her mental camera makes.

"Now turn around," Mrs. Kane said.

Cam turned around.

"What do you remember?"

Mrs. Kane asked.

"You have curly white hair," Cam said.

"Your dress has four buttons.

You're holding a purple cane

with a silver handle.

On the chair next to you

is a large leather bag.

Just under the handle of the bag

are the three letters 'M S K.'"

"The letters are for my name,
Mary Sharon Kane," Mrs. Kane said.
"And you do have an amazing
memory."
Cam turned around.
"Now," Danny asked.
"Who knows what's green and jumpy?"
No one answered.
"It's a leaf with hiccups," Danny said.
No one laughed.
"Let's go," Eric said.
Cam, Eric, and Danny
went into the gym to see the fair.

Chapter 2
Speedy Is Gone!

There were lots of tables in the gym.

Each was covered with a cloth.

There were signs explaining what we

can do to keep our earth green.

Lots of children were walking

from one table to the next.

"Try my car.

Try my car," a boy called out.

"It's electric."

He gave Eric a remote-control unit.

"Push the button," the boy said.

There was a toy car on the floor.

Eric pushed the button.

The car moved forward.

"Push the button again," the boy

said, "and look for smoke."

Eric pushed it again,

but there was no smoke.

"My name is Ben," he told

Cam and Eric.

"My car's name is Speedy.

"Inside Speedy is a small battery.

That's electricity.

Cars that use gas fill the air

with smoke.

Electric cars don't."

"Thank you," Cam and Eric said.

"Hello," the girl at the next table

called out.

"My name is Paula."

On the table were a small windmill,

a lamp, and two bicycle pumps.

"Wind energy is clean energy,"
Paula said very loudly.
"Wind can light our homes."
Paula held one bicycle pump
near the windmill.
She gave the other one to Eric.
"Let's turn those blades," she said.
Paula and Eric pumped.
The moving air turned the blades.
When the blades turned,
the light went on.

Danny said, "Let me try that."

He pointed the pump at Cam.

He blew air in her face.

"Hey," Cam said. "Stop that."

"Help me!" Ben called.

"Help me!

Speedy is gone!"

Cam pushed the hair from her eyes.

She turned to look at Ben's electric
car display.

Ms. Dee and Mrs. Kane were there.

But Speedy was gone.

Chapter 3
Cam Says, "Click!"

Cam, Eric, and Danny

went to Ben's table.

Cam looked at the table.

She blinked her eyes and said, "Click!"

Cam looked at the chair

next to the table.

She blinked her eyes again

and said, "Click!"

Each time Cam looked at something,

she blinked her eyes and said, "Click!"

Eric told Ben, "When Cam clicks

she solves mysteries.

My friend Cam will find your car."

"No, she won't," Danny said.

"I'll solve the mystery."

Danny looked around.

"There are just two ways

out of this place," he said.

"The way we came in and those doors."

Danny pointed to the red doors

at the far end of the gym.

"Here's what the thief did."

Danny took Mrs. Kane's bag

off the chair.

He put it under his shirt

and walked toward the red doors.

"Hey," Mrs. Kane said.

"Give that back."

Danny turned.

He put the bag on the table.

"I gave you your bag back," Danny

said, "but the thief who stole Ben's

car isn't giving it back."

"Oh, yes he is," Ben said.

He hurried toward the red doors.

Eric and Danny followed him.

Cam looked at Ms. Dee and Mrs. Kane.

She looked at the table.

She looked at the two chairs.

On one chair was the remote.

Cam looked at the floor

where Speedy had been.

Cam blinked her eyes and said, "Click!"

Then she hurried to the red doors

at the far end of the gym.

Chapter 4
The Math Teacher Has Problems

"I'm Jane," a girl called to Cam. She was standing by a table near the red doors.

"Let me show you how important it is to insulate your home."

"Did anyone go out through these doors?" Cam asked.

"Yes," Jane said.

"Ben and two boys just left."

"Did anyone else leave?" Cam asked.

"I didn't see anyone else," Jane said.

"But I wasn't always watching.

Sometimes I was telling people

about insulation.

It saves energy."

Cam opened one of the red doors.

She looked across the school

parking lot.

Cam saw Ben, Eric, and Danny.

She saw lots of cars.

But these were full-sized cars.

None of the cars was Speedy.

Ben, Eric, and Danny

walked back into the gym.

Cam held the door open for them.

"Do you know why the math teacher

was sad?" Danny asked.

"I don't want to hear jokes,"

Ben told Danny.

"I want to find Speedy."

"He was sad because he had

so many problems."

Ben put his hands to his ears.

"Can't anyone stop him?" Ben asked.

"Just one more.

What's yellow and goes on the highway without a driver?

It's a remote-controlled banana."

"*What* is it?" Cam asked.

"It's a remote-controlled banana," Danny said again.

"Oh my!" Cam told Danny.

"I think you helped me find Speedy."

"I did?" Danny said.

Cam looked across the gym.

She closed her eyes and said, "Click!"

Cam said, "Click!" again.

Then she opened her eyes.

"I don't think anyone
stole your car," she told Ben.

"And I think I know where
to find Speedy."

Chapter 5
Do You Want to Hear Another Joke?

"How did I help solve the mystery?" Danny asked.

Cam laughed.

"It was your banana joke," she said. "I remembered that Speedy is gone, but the remote is still on the chair."

"Why would anyone take Speedy and leave the remote?" Eric said.

"If I'm right," Cam said, "no one took Speedy."

Cam, Eric, Ben, and Danny
walked toward Ben's table.
Ms. Dee and Mrs. Kane
were at Paula's wind energy table.
Eric told them, "I think Cam is
going to solve another mystery."
Ms. Dee and Mrs. Kane
went with Cam and the others
to Ben's electric car table.
"Your bag must be heavy,"
Cam said to Mrs. Kane.

"Yes," Mrs. Kane said.

"I'm an old woman.

It's hard to carry this heavy bag."

Cam said, "Why don't you put it down?"

Mrs. Kane put her bag on the chair.

Bzzzz! Bzzzz! Bzzzz!

"Do you hear that?" Cam asked.

Eric said, "I don't hear anything.

It's too noisy in here."

Cam stood near Ben's table.

She bent down.

"Listen here," she said.

Eric, Danny, and Ben

stood near the table and listened.

Bzzzz! Bzzzz! Bzzzz!

"Now I hear it," Eric said.

Ben lifted the cloth.

"There you are!" Ben said.

He crawled under the table.

When he crawled out,

he had Speedy.

The toy car's wheels were turning.

"Your bag did it," Cam told Mrs. Kane.

Cam lifted Mrs. Kane's bag,

and Speedy's wheels stopped turning.

"When Ben said 'Speedy is gone,'

we all came to look for Speedy.

Your bag was on the chair.

It was on top of the remote.

You put your bag on the remote

and sent Speedy under the table.

Speedy hit the wall and stopped."

Danny said, "It was my joke that helped Cam solve the mystery."

"Yes, it was," Cam said.

Danny asked, "Do you want to hear another joke?"

"No," Ben said.

Eric said, "I want to see what I can do to keep our earth green."

"Good," Mrs. Kane said.

"I hope the earth will still be green when you're old like me."

"Me too," Cam said.

"And I hope to have white curly hair just like yours."

A Cam Jansen Memory Game

Take another look at the picture on page 4.
Study it.
Blink your eyes and say, "Click!"
Then turn back to this page
and answer these questions:

1. Is Cam smiling?

2. Mrs. Kane is the old woman.
   What color is her dress?

3. What color is Mrs. Kane's cane?

4. Where is Mrs. Kane's large leather
   bag?

5. Are any of the children wearing
   striped shirts?

6. Are there more than 10 children
   in the picture?